Where Are All The Minnesotans?

Written by **Karlyn Coleman**

Illustrated by **Carrie Hartman**

MINNESOTA HISTORICAL SOCIETY PRESS

Where are all the Minnesotans?
Is it too cold to go outside?

No!
Snow pants, a jacket,
a pair of warm boots,
wool mittens on your hands,
a hat pulled over your ears,
a scarf covering your nose,
and off you go.

Where are all the Minnesotans? Is it too cold to go fishing?

No! It's nice and snug in a little fishing house.
Auger a hole, tie on an orange bobber,
drop a line, and wait for a walleye to bite.

Where are all the Minnesotans? Is it too cold to skate?
No! It's a perfect day for a pond hockey game.

Shovel off a rink, tie on some skates, and race
back and forth across smooth, shiny ice,
passing the puck until a goal is scored.

Where are all the Minnesotans?
Is it too cold for a parade?

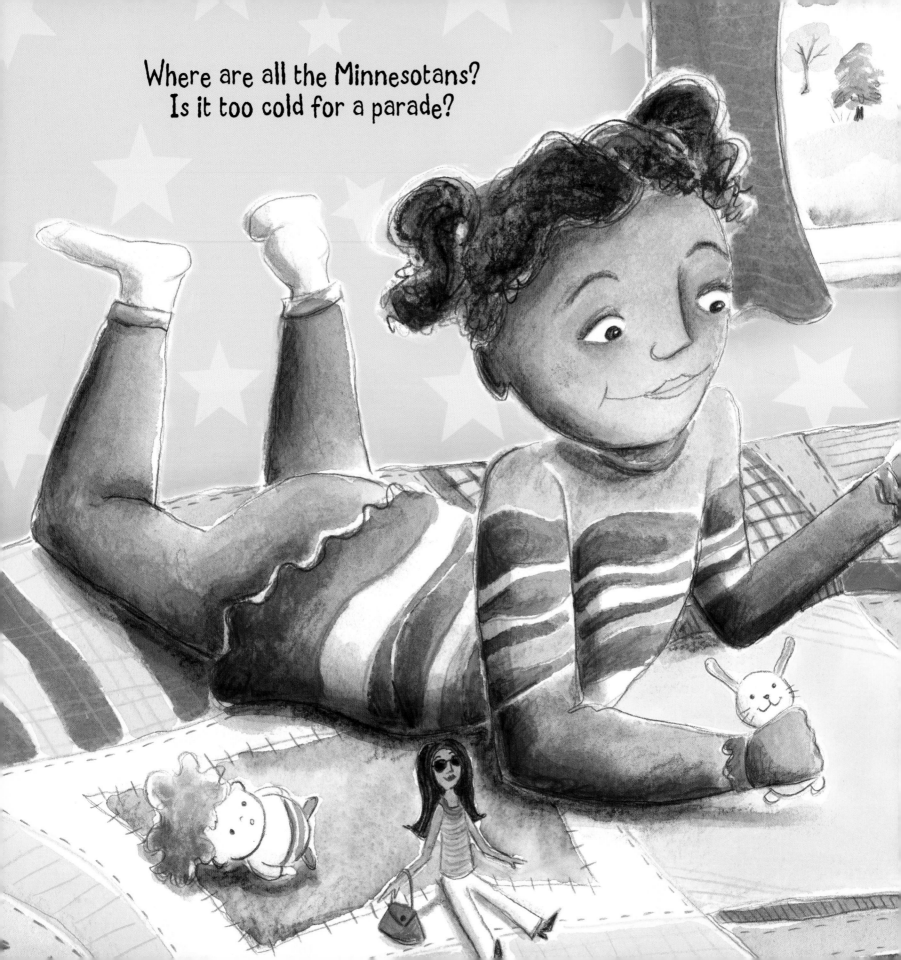

No!
Here comes King Boreas
leading the way.

Music and laughter melt
the ice off the streets,
and a winter carnival makes
a chilly city feel warm.

Where are all the Minnesotans?
Is it too cold to fly a kite?

No!
A frozen lake is the perfect place: no trees,
no wires, just wide-open space, and a strong
north wind to push bright-colored kites up and
up toward clouds ready to burst with snow.

Where are all the Minnesotans?
Does the early-setting sun keep
everyone from going out?

No!
Candles flicker and glow along ski trails,
and the moon and stars shine down from above,
everything so clear and bright
on a beautiful winter night.

Where are all the Minnesotans? Is the snow too deep?
No! Grab a shovel, hook up the plow,
and when a path is clear, gather up friends
and sled down white-covered hills.

Where are all the Minnesotans?
The temperature has dropped to thirty below,
the wind is blowing, and the schools are closed.

Now all the Minnesotans are gathered inside,
reading books, baking sweet treats,
building roaring fires in the fireplace.

And what all these Minnesotans know is that
soon the ice and snow will melt away,
and when spring comes, no one will have to ask,

"Where are all the Minnesotans?"

Because everyone will be outside.

The Minnesota Historical Society Press is a member of the Association
of American University Presses.
Manufactured in Malaysia
10 9 8 7 6 5 4 3 2 1

♾ The paper used in this publication meets the minimum requirements of
the American National Standard for Information Sciences—
Permanence for Printed Library Materials, ANSI Z39.48-1984.

International Standard Book Number   ISBN: 978-1-68134-040-1
Library of Congress Cataloging-in-Publication Data
available upon request.

Dedicated to:
Auggie, Alex, and Elaine Rose,
who all love ice and snow. —KC

Dedicated to:
Ken and Dianne,
two of my favorite Minnesotans. —CH